Outdoor Art Activities

Jonathon Phillips
Photographs by Lindsay Edwards

Contents

Art Outside

Drawing, painting and sculpting are fun art activities to do. Most of the time, these activities are done inside the classroom, but they can be just as enjoyable to do outside. The light outside is brighter, so the artist can see things more clearly. An artist can make amazing art by looking at different things outside, such as the trees, shadows, clouds and animals.

Artists can also draw in sand with sticks, or shape sand into beautiful sculptures. They can draw with charcoal or chalk on concrete paths. There are so many things an artist can use instead of a pen and paper.

Here are three art activities that can be done outside.

DARIA
JUDE

A Very Colourful Tree

Trees are wonderful to draw. They come in many different sizes, shapes and colours. If you are ever unsure about what to draw, go outside and look at a tree.

Look closely at the leaves of the tree. What colour are they? Are they green? What shade of green are they? You will see that leaves can be many different shades of green. The same tree could have light-green, dark-green, blue-green and lime-coloured leaves.

Goal

To make a picture of a tree with brilliant leaves of different colours

Materials

You will need:

- a clipboard

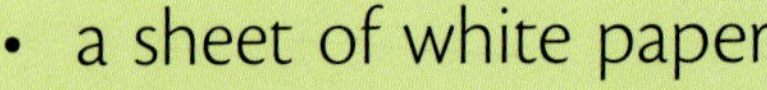

- a sheet of white paper

- a pencil
- oil pastels

- a cap of blue food dye mixed into a glass of water

- a paintbrush.

Steps

1. Choose a tree to draw. Make sure it has lots of leaves. Find a comfortable place to sit where you can clearly see the tree.

2. Place the sheet of paper on the clipboard. Using the pencil, draw a curved line across the page, near the bottom. This will be the ground.
3. Draw the tree trunk.

4. Draw the thicker branches coming from the trunk of the tree.
5. Add some smaller branches.

6. Look at the shape of the leaves on the tree you chose. The leaves could be shaped like ovals, circles, teardrops or something similar. Decide which is the right shape, then draw leaves all around the branches of your tree.

7. You will need to go inside the classroom to finish your picture.

   Use a brown oil pastel to colour in the tree trunk. Then, colour the branches brown, too.

8. Separate the green oil pastels from the other colours. Put the green oil pastels to one side.

9. Colour in all the leaves. Use different-coloured oil pastels, including white. Do not use any green pastels.

10. Now, use the different green oil pastels to colour over each leaf a second time.

11. Colour in the ground. Draw some green grass and fallen leaves on the ground.

12. With a white oil pastel, write your name on the side of your paper. You will not see it yet, but you will be able to see it later on.

13. Paint over the whole page with the mixture of blue food dye and water. The food dye and the oil pastels will react to each other. You will be able to see the different green colours as well as all the other bright colours. You will also be able to see your name, when you paint over it. Remember to place a sheet of paper under your painting before adding the dye and water.

14. Wait for your painting to dry.

Your tree of many different colours is finished!

A Chalk Shadow Drawing

Sidewalk art is an unusual art form. Wind blows over it, people walk on it and the rain washes it away. It will not last forever, but you can enjoy doing it all again.

Using chalk is a great way to create big outdoor artworks. All you need is some large chalk, a hard surface such as a concrete path and an object to draw.

Goal

To create a shadow drawing with chalk

Materials

You will need:

- sidewalk chalk
- an object with an interesting shape, such as a bike or a chair
- a concrete path or area where there is plenty of sunshine.

Steps

1. Look for a concrete path or area in the sunshine.
2. Place your object on the concrete so that it casts a shadow across the area where you want to draw.

3. Choose a piece of chalk. Carefully trace around the edge of the shadow. Make sure you go around all the details.

4. Stand back and look at your work. Have you outlined everything? Is there anything you have missed?

5. Once you are happy with the tracing, remove the object so you can see your outline without the shadow.

6. Colour in the shape. Spread the colour around by smudging the chalk.

7. Add highlights and shadows by smudging white and coloured chalk over some areas. Add white chalk on the top parts and the coloured chalk on the lower parts of the drawing.

8. Sign your work.

A Sandpit Sculpture

You don't have to go to the beach to make a sand sculpture. A sandpit, some water and a few simple tools are all you need to make a great piece of outdoor art.

Goal

To make a sculpture of a head with sand and objects that you can find around the schoolyard

Materials

You will need:

- a sandpit
- a stick

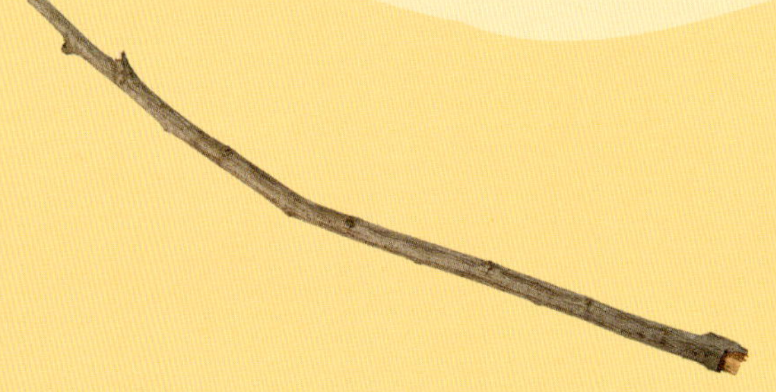

- a bucket
- a large bottle of water
- a plastic spoon
- a paintbrush
- some leaves, stones and flowers.

Steps

1. Level and smooth out an area of sand.
2. Use the stick to mark out a large oval shape.

3. Fill one third of the bucket with sand.
4. Add some water to the bucket. Then, mix the sand and water together until all the sand is damp.

5. Scoop up a handful of damp sand from the bucket. Pat it into the shape of an egg. Place the sand egg inside the oval shape. Repeat until the oval is filled with three layers of sand eggs.

6. Gently pat down the sand eggs and smooth out the gaps, until you have one large oval-shaped dome.

7. Use the stick to lightly mark a line across the centre of the dome from left to right. Mark another line down the centre from top to bottom.
8. Using the plastic spoon, carve out two eye sockets.

9. Shape some sand into a nose. Start between the eyes and finish when you are halfway to the chin. Take the stick and make two holes for nostrils.

10. With your stick, make a smiling mouth.

11. Use the paintbrush to smooth out the head and the area around it.

12. Decorate the face with your objects. Use stones for eyes and leaves for hair and eyebrows.

If you have time, you could make a body for your head. But remember that your sand sculpture will not last a long time. The wind will wear it down, rain will wash it away or little feet will trample over it.